FNB

D0800041

Books by Jacqueline Wilson

MARK SPARK IN THE DARK
TAKE A GOOD LOOK
VIDEO ROSE
THE WEREPUPPY
THE WEREPUPPY ON HOLIDAY

JACQUELINE WILSON

STARRING

MARK SPARK AND VIDEO ROSE

ILLUSTRATED BY
JANET ROBERTSON
AND BETHAN MATTHEWS

PUFFIN

PUFFIN BOOKS

Published by the Penguin Group
Penguin Books Ltd, 80 Strand, London WC2R 0RL, England
Penguin Group (USA) Inc., 375 Hudson Street, New York, New York 10014, USA
Penguin Books Australia Ltd, 250 Camberwell Road, Camberwell, Victoria 3124, Australia
Penguin Books Canada Ltd, 10 Alcorn Avenue, Toronto, Ontario, Canada M4V 3B2
Penguin Books India (P) Ltd, 11 Community Centre, Panchsheel Park, New Delhi – 110 017, India
Penguin Group (NZ), cnr Airborne and Rosedale Roads, Albany, Auckland 1310, New Zealand
Penguin Books (South Africa) (Pty) Ltd, 24 Sturdee Avenue, Rosebank 2196, South Africa

Penguin Books Ltd, Registered Offices: 80 Strand, London WC2R 0RL, England

www.penguin.com

Video Rose first published by Blackie Children's Books 1992
Video Rose first published in Puffin Books 1994
Mark Spark in the Dark first published by Hamish Hamilton 1993
Mark Spark in the Dark first published in Puffin Books 1994
First published in one volume 2005
009

Video Rose text copyright © Jacqueline Wilson, 1992, 2005
Mark Spark in the Dark text copyright © Jacqueline Wilson, 1993, 2005
Video Rose illustrations copyright © Janet Robertson, 1992, 2005
Mark Spark in the Dark illustrations copyright © Bethan Matthews, 1993, 2005
All rights reserved

The moral right of the author and illustrators has been asserted

Made and printed in England by Clays Ltd, St Ives plc

British Library Cataloguing in Publication Data
A CIP catalogue record for this book is available from the British Library

ISBN 0–141–31949–6

www.greenpenguin.co.uk

Penguin Books is committed to a sustainable
future for our business, our readers and our planet.
This book is made from Forest Stewardship
Council™ certified paper.

ALWAYS LEARNING   **PEARSON**

Contents

Video Rose   1

Mark Spark   89

Mark Spark in the Dark   131

VIDEO ROSE

Her right hand was glowing like a little
electric fire. She was suddenly jolted
forward, swooping through the table,
through the flat, through time itself. She
seemed to be hurtling on forever . . .

1...

'You'll get square eyes watching videos all day long,' said Mum.

'I don't care,' said Rose, juggling her video collection. Did she want to watch *The Wizard of Oz* for the five hundredth time?

'Square eyes to match her square shape,' said Rick, tying up his new roller-skates.

Rose ignored him, mumbling the Munchkin song to herself, but when he tottered past the television she stuck out her leg.

'Rick!' said Mum as he went sprawling. 'I've told you not to wear those things in the house.'

'It wasn't my fault, Mum, old Square-Belly stuck her great fat leg out on purpose,' said Rick.

'Don't you *dare* call me Square-Belly!' Rose shrieked, attacking him with her *Tom and Jerry* video.

'Rose, stop it! Calm down both of you, you'll wake your Dad. Rose, did you hear me? Stop bashing your brother. Although really Rick, I absolutely forbid you to call your sister Square-Belly ever again.'

'OK, OK. Ouch!' said Rick, grabbing one of Mum's aerobic exercise videos and making it whizz energetically in his defence. 'Stop it, Rose. I won't ever call you Square-Belly again. Square-Bum suits you much better!'

'I'll get you for that!' Rose roared, picking up *Pretty Woman* in her other hand and attacking him on both sides.

'Rose, cut it out! That's not even ours, I hired it from Uncle Frank,' said Mum, snatching *Pretty Woman* from Plain Girl.

Baby Robbie started squawking in his baby chair, flinging his little arms and legs around. It wouldn't be long before he was joining in the fights too.

'Honestly, you're like wild animals, all three of you,' said Mum, separating Rose and Rick and then struggling with Robbie's straps. 'Come on, Robbie, we've got to get going.'

Robbie stopped squawking. He went red in the face, concentrating.

'Oh no,' Mum moaned. 'Have I got to change your nappy again? I'm going to be late for work.'

It was the half-term holidays but Mum still had to go out to work in the shop during the day, same as Dad had to go out to the factory at night. Robbie went with Mum and stayed in the crèche while Mum served the customers. Rose and Rick were big enough to look after themselves, and they could always wake Dad in an emergency. Dad worked the night shift and slept right through the morning, so long as there wasn't too much noise going on in the rest of the flat.

'You two have got to *behave*,' said Mum, laying Robbie on the floor and hurriedly unpopping his dungarees.

'Yuck,' said Rick, holding his nose. He'd been longing for a little brother but he didn't rate him very highly so far. 'I'm going out.'

'Don't roller-skate up and down the balconies, you go to the playground, do you hear me?' said Mum. 'Why don't you go to the playground too, Rose?'

'I don't like it down that playground, it's boring,' said Rose. 'I'd sooner stay in and watch videos.'

'You'll turn into a video yourself one day,' said Mum. 'Here, will you take *Pretty Woman* back for me?'

'Can I hire a new video, Mum? Oh go on, Mum please. Give us two pounds, eh?' Rose wheedled.

'Look, this is ridiculous, I'm not made of money,' said Mum, swabbing at Robbie's bottom. 'Hold still, you silly little sausage. Oh no! Rose, run and see if you can find a clean pair of dungarees for him, eh?'

'OK Mum. And I'll fetch the nappies. And I'll get all the clothes out the washing machine and fold them ready for ironing. Gosh, I'm such a help to you, aren't I, Mum? I don't know what you'd do without me. So how about showing a little gratitude, eh? Two weeny teeny little pound coins for a video?' said Rose, going down on her knees, pretending to beg.

'You're a shocker, you are,' said Mum, swabbing at Robbie. 'All right then, get the money out of my purse.'

Rick was halfway out the front door, but he came zooming back indignantly.

'That's not fair, Mum! Why can't I have two pounds too? Everyone else goes down to Macdonalds for their lunch so why can't I have the money to go and all? Oh Mum, please, don't be mean.'

Poor Mum wasn't a bit mean. She ended up being extremely generous before rushing off to work with a freshly-changed Robbie. Rick skated happily up and down the balconies, jingling the coins in his pocket. And Rose had a long happy browse in Uncle Frank's video shop, sorting out her selection for the day. She was in luck. Uncle Frank was running a special promotion. All the children's videos were down to one pound fifty per hire. Of course these were really babyish films. They weren't meant for sophisticated girls like Rose. But no one need know. And then she'd have fifty pence extra to spend. She could afford a bag of salt and vinegar crisps and a pack of pink and white marshmallows as well. Mum was always going on at her about a balanced diet. Well, she was balancing salty and sweet.

She went back to the flat clutching her chosen video and her bonus snacks, dodging the demon roller skater on the way. She popped her head round the door of Dad's bedroom. He was sleeping like a baby. Rose giggled. Robbie was a real baby but he hadn't done much sleeping at all yet. Mum was generally up and down all night. Maybe Dad was on to a good thing working on the night shift.

Rose shut the door on Dad, went into the living room and slotted the video into the machine. She loved the little whirring noise it made, the click and then the hiss as it started spooling round when she pressed the play button. She settled herself comfortably on the sofa, using her tummy as a table for the bag of crisps and the marshmallows. *Dumbo* flickered into action.

'B-l-i-s-s,' said Rose, taking a mouthful of crisps and then another mouthful of marshmallows.

It was going to be fun seeing dear old Dumbo again. If Rick came barging back he'd scoff at her choice. He never watched baby cartoons. He said they were just for little kiddiewinks. Rick and his mates all watched horror videos. Rose had watched some too. Well she hadn't exactly *watched*. She'd had her hands over her eyes most of the time. She had begged Rick to fast forward through the really gruesome parts but Rick said they were the best bits. Mum had eventually caught them both scrunched up on the sofa watching a monster movie where a head exploded in slow motion. Mum had exploded in very fast motion and thrown the video in the rubbish bin. She had acted like she wanted to throw Rick in the rubbish bin too.

Rose giggled again, scrunching crisps and sucking marshmallows. She kept jumping up and down off the sofa to press the rewind button so she could watch her favourite scenes over and over again. Rose never watched a video straight though. Well, she did when Mum was around, because Mum kept nagging at her that she was going to break their video machine if she didn't watch out. It was an ancient old thing and one day they'd have a brand new video recorder with all sorts of interesting controls and Rose could barely wait — but just now there wasn't any spare cash so they had to make do with this old junky video that looked positively Victorian. Only they didn't have videos in Victorian times. Not even televisions. Rose couldn't work out what they did with themselves in those long-ago days. Mum said they went out to play and got a bit of exercise. Well, Rose got her exercise bounding up from the sofa and back again to press the rewind button.

She swallowed the last of the crisps and licked the inside of the bag. Then she experimented with the marshmallows, seeing if she could tell the pink taste from the white. It was interesting seeing how many marshmallows she could cram into her mouth at one

time. But then they were gone in a gulp. Rose sighed sadly.

Poor Dumbo looked down-hearted too. It was getting to the bit where Mrs Jumbo is shut up and Dumbo can't get at her. Rose always got a bit sniffly when they twined trunks. She leapt up to fast forward through this bit. Her fingers were sticky and salty and slipped on the video controls. She pressed both the fast forward and the rewind buttons by accident. The video buzzed in protest and then Dumbo and Mrs Jumbo and their twining trunks disappeared.

'Oh crumbs,' said Rose, her heart beating fast. She tried pressing the play button. Nothing happened. She took the video out the machine. At least it wasn't all mangled up with the tape flapping. She tried slotting it back and pressing the play button again. No, it wouldn't work. She tried *The Wizard of Oz*. 'Please play for me,' she said, in a good witch Glinda voice. But it wouldn't play.

'Oh crumbs,' Rose repeated, kneeling in front of the video. 'Oh more than crumbs. Oh slices of bread. Oh zonking great loaves.'

She stood up on trembling legs, trying not to cry. She staggered out of the living room and into Mum and Dad's bedroom.

'Dad. Oh Dad. Wake up, Dad.'

Dad was snuggled right down under the duvet, just a few tufts of his hair showing. He snuggled further down at the sound of her voice.

'Dad, please! Dad! DAD!'

Dad peered out with one eye open. His face was screwed up. He looked rumpled and cross.

'What is it?' he mumbled.

'Oh Dad, it's so awful,' said Rose, tears starting to dribble down her cheeks.

Dad sat straight up in bed, blinking.

'What's awful? What's happened, Rose? Have you hurt yourself? Is it Rick? Quick, love, tell me!'

'It's broken,' Rose wailed.

'What's broken? Rick's arm, Rick's leg? I *knew* those stupid skates were a mistake,' said Dad scrambling out of bed.

'It's not Rick, it's not me, it's the video,' said Rose.

'The video?' said Dad, pausing.

'Yes, the video's broken, I've tried and tried, but it won't work, and it's not my fault, I

swear it isn't, it just went sort of phut
and —'

Dad seemed to be going sort of phut too. He
sighed several times. He took a very deep
breath. Then he got back into bed and pulled
the duvet over his head.

'*Dad*?' said Rose.

'Go away,' said Dad. It sounded as if his
teeth were clenched.

'But Dad —'

'Rose. Let me get back to sleep. Look, I
thought you knew by now. You mustn't ever
wake me up unless there's a terrible emergency.'

Rose stared at Dad under the duvet, utterly
amazed. She didn't understand. Rose thought
the video breaking *was* the worst emergency
ever.

2...

Dad wouldn't wake up properly and get someone to come to fix the video.

'But we've got to get it fixed,' said Rose desperately.

'*I'll* fix it for you, no bother,' said Rick, limping in with torn jeans and bloody knees.

'Are they your new jeans? Mum's going to do her nut,' said Rose.

'Well, wait till she knows you've busted the video,' said Rick, taking off his roller skates and dabbing gingerly at his knees. 'Ouch!'

'I didn't bust it. It bust itself. Oh Rick, do you really think you could mend it?' said Rose.

Rick might fancy himself as a Mr Fix-It but he didn't often have much luck. He was good at taking things to bits to find out why they were broken. He wasn't always so great at putting things back together, mended. But he had once managed to slot the legs back on a Barbie doll, and he had very nearly mended an alarm clock, though it rattled rather than

rang. Perhaps he could somehow get the video working again. Rose decided it didn't matter too much about the fast forward and the rewind button. She'd learn to live without them. Just so long as she could press the play button and get the video running then she'd rest content.

Rick knelt on his sore knee and unscrewed little bits of the video and peered at them, muttering to himself.

'Are you sure you know what you're doing?' Rose asked anxiously.

'Of course I'm sure,' said Rick, but he didn't sound it. He twiddled and fiddled. He pressed the fast forward button. He pressed the rewind button. He pressed the play button. Nothing happened.

'This video's busted,' said Rick.

'I know that!' said Rose. 'That's why you're mending it.'

But Rick couldn't mend it. He couldn't even get all the bits to go back properly. The slot for the video slanted alarmingly, and several screws stuck out.

'Oh, Rick! Look what you've done!' said Rose.

'It's not *my* fault,' said Rick. 'I didn't bust it in the first place.'

They were still arguing about it when Dad got up in the afternoon. He was a bit grumpy, and he got grumpier still when reminded about the broken video. He had a look at it himself and shook his head.

'Can't you mend it, Dad?' said Rose.

'Sorry, pal. It's been on its last legs for ages.'

Rose looked at the broken old video. She imagined it on a pair of bandy old legs, tottering, stumbling, falling flat. Then far away in the distance she pictured a new modern video running about athletically on sleek muscled legs.

'Could we buy a new video then?' Rose asked desperately.

Dad shook his head again. 'What with? Peanuts?'

'But we could pay it off monthly,' Rose said, while the imaginary video ran right past her.

'We're paying off too much as it is,' said Dad. He sounded miserable. He'd been out of work for a while before he got the night shift job at the factory. Mum had had to go back to

15

work full time after Robbie was born. Rose knew Dad always got touchy when they talked about money, but she was feeling frantic.

'Couldn't we get a new video and pay off just a bit more?' she said.

'No! You kids, you never stop. You've got to have all these silly trendy clothes and trainers that cost a fortune and blooming roller skates for your birthday —'

'*I* didn't get roller-skates for my birthday,' said Rose, although she knew it wasn't wise to argue with Dad right this minute.

Dad got cross. There was a bit of a row. Rick cleared off to do some more roller-skating though he was limping worse than ever. Rose sat hunched in a corner of the sofa. The television itself was still working but there was nothing she felt like watching. She kept looking mournfully at the poor broken-down video.

Dad sighed. He phoned up one of his mates who was also on the night shift and asked him if his father-in-law still did television and video repairs. The mate said yes, but he had such a lot of sets in his garage waiting to be

mended that it would be weeks before he could get round to it. Maybe months.

'Still, he'll maybe be able to fix it, and he won't charge very much,' said Dad.

'He said it would take weeks, Dad. Maybe months,' said Rose, who had sharp ears. 'I can't wait *months*!'

Dad felt she was being ungrateful and got tetchy again. Rick came back rubbing his elbows with a tear in his sweatshirt. Mum came home from the shop with Robbie yelling his head off for his feed.

Tea was not a happy meal. Mum went on and on about the video, saying that she'd *told* Rose not to keep fiddling about with the buttons. It was as if Mum was continuously rewinding her own button. Rose wished there was some way of fast-forwarding her until she stopped being cross.

Mum was much more sympathetic in the morning.

'Cheer up, Rosy-Posy. I can't bear to see you with such a long face,' said Mum, sorting clothes for the washing machine.

Rose was so wretched she felt her face getting longer and longer. It would droop right down to her knees at this rate.

'What am I going to *do* all day?' she wailed. 'It was so awful yesterday when I only got to watch half of *Dumbo*.'

'A broken video isn't the end of the world, you know,' Mum said gently, looking at a pair of jeans. She put her hands down both legs and stuck her fingers through both knees. 'Rick!' She didn't sound anywhere near so gentle now. 'Rick, these are your new jeans!'

'Can't we get someone in to mend the video, Mum?' Rose begged.

'Dad said there's a man at work — oh no! Look at this sweatshirt! Richard Michael, get yourself into the kitchen this instant. I want an explanation.'

Rick's explanation wasn't very satisfactory. Mum said he wasn't allowed to go skating today. Rick argued indignantly. Mum got cross. Baby Robbie got cross too and started yelling in his little chair. Dad got cross as well, because he hadn't got to sleep yet and he didn't know how he was expected to with everyone bellowing like bulls.

'I'm not bellowing,' Rose mumbled miserably and went to fiddle with the video.

'You're wasting your time, Rose,' Mum said, but before she hurried off to work she looked up the number of a television and video repair business. She phoned them. They said they could come out to look at the video that afternoon. Rose leapt high in the air for joy. She came down with rather a crash but she didn't care. They could come and fix the video.

No, they couldn't. They were doubtful for a start when Mum told them the make and age of the video and how it wouldn't work at all. They said they'd still come and see, but of course there would be a call-out charge. And then they charged an hourly rate for any work involved. Rose heard the vast sums and slumped back on the sofa.

'I'm afraid we can't afford that,' said Mum, and put down the phone. She shook her head sadly at Rose. 'I'm sorry, love, but it would be crazy to spend a small fortune — and there's no guarantee at all they could actually fix the video.'

Mum went off to work with Robbie. Rick waited a minute or two, and then slung his skates round his neck and sauntered towards the front door.

'Mum said you're not allowed to skate!' said Rose.

'I'm not skating, am I ?' said Rick.

'Oh, I get it, you're just *wearing* them today,' said Rose.

'That's right. I'm getting very fashion conscious. This is my dead stylish chunky necklace,' said Rick, waving his arms and swivelling his hips like a model.

Rose listened after he went out the front door. There was a long pause. And then she heard the swoosh of little wheels along the concrete. It looked like Rick's new necklace was now taking him for a ride.

She actually caught him at it when she went out to the shops to return the *Dumbo* video.

'I'm telling Mum,' Rose shouted. She probably wouldn't tell, but she wanted to make Rick squirm a bit.

'You shut your face, Square-Bum,' Rick shouted back, and his mate Charlie chortled delightedly.

Rose decided she would definitely tell Mum after all. She stumped off to Uncle Frank's.

'What's up with you, Rose? You look a bit fed up,' said Uncle Frank.

'A bit!' said Rose. 'Oh Uncle Frank, our video's broken and I don't know what to do. It went kerphut right in the middle of *Dumbo*. I couldn't rewind it. I do hope the tape's OK.' She handed it over nervously. If it was broken then she'd have to save up her pocket money for ages to pay for it.

Uncle Frank tried the tape on his own machine and Dumbo danced back into action.

'Phew!' said Rose. She watched the screen. 'Can I stay for a bit, Uncle Frank?'

Uncle Frank laughed. 'OK. You can stay all morning if you help me sort all the videos on the racks, they're in an awful mess. Are you getting your own set fixed today?'

'No, we can't afford it,' said Rose, drooping.

'Well, did you see the card in my window? This nice old chap seems to have started up his own business.'

Rose ran outside the shop to look at the card in the window.

TROUBLED WITH THE
TELEVISION?
VEXED WITH THE VIDEO?
I CAN FIX THEM AT VERY
FAVOURABLE RATES.

NO CALL OUT CHARGE.

There was a telephone number. And the name of the firm. It sounded promising:

WORKS-LIKE-MAGIC.

3...

Rose brought Dad breakfast in bed. She ran a bath for him. She played his favourite old Elvis tape while he was getting dressed.

'It's no use, Rosy-Posy,' said Dad. 'I can't get you a new video.'

'I know, Dad. But there's this new business for fixing videos. WORKS-LIKE-MAGIC.'

'It would need to,' said Dad, but after he'd had a second cup of coffee he rang the number.

The man at the other end said he'd be right with them, in two shakes of a lamb's tail.

Rose picked up Robbie's toy lamb which was grazing peacefully in a dusty corner of the carpet. She tweaked the fluffy tail twice — and immediately there was a very loud ring at the door.

Rose and Dad looked at each other.

'It can't be this bloke already,' said Dad.

'It must be,' said Rose, dashing to the door.

There was a strange old man standing on the doorstep. He looked as if he'd just got up

from his bed too. His white hair stuck straight up in the air and the crumpled blue and white striped trousers showing beneath his big raincoat looked suspiciously like pyjamas.

His eyes sparkled when he saw Rose and he gave her a flashing smile.

'I believe you require my services, young lady,' he said.

'I want you to mend our video, please,' said Rose.

'Oh, is that all,' said the strange man. 'Just as you please.'

Dad edged up behind Rose.

'Could you give us some idea of your charges first, if you don't mind,' Dad asked.

'A pound a minute,' said the strange man.

'Well in that case we'll have to part company,' said Dad. 'Your rates are far too expensive.'

'Oh, Dad!' said Rose desperately.

'Now look, Rose, it's going to take hours and hours to get that video working again, if indeed it's possible. We simply can't afford it,' Dad hissed.

'I'll just take a look,' said the strange man. He walked briskly into the living room. There was a crackling sound as he moved. Perhaps his raincoat was made of some odd material. He bent down and squinted at the video.

'I can mend this in a flash,' said the strange man, and he reached out and touched the video with the tip of his finger.

There was a sudden jagged white flash, like lightning. Rose jumped, Dad gasped, and the strange man sucked his teeth in a sizzly sort of way.

'Here, watch out!' said Dad, going to grab the man. 'That video must be live.'

'Yes, I've livened it up for you,' said the strange man, straightening swiftly and ducking away from Dad. 'It's fully fixed now.'

'But — but it can't be,' said Dad.

'Oh yes it is,' said the strange man, and he slotted in *The Wizard of Oz* and pressed the play button.

It started playing immediately. The strange man pressed the fast forward button. The tape whizzed forward to the bright colour of Munchkin land. He pressed the rewind button. The tape zapped Dorothy back to black and white Kansas.

'See. Fully working. Care to try it, sir?' said the strange man.

Dad had a go at the controls himself. His hand was shaking as he pressed the buttons.

'You said you'd mend it in a flash,' Rose whispered, awestruck. 'And that's just what you did.'

'That's right, my dear,' said the strange man. He consulted a large watch on his wrist. 'We won't quibble over a few seconds. You owe me a pound for my services, sir.'

'But — but — but I can't just pay you a pound,' Dad stammered. 'It's nowhere near enough.'

The strange man sucked his teeth again, sounding even more sizzly.

'You seemed to think my rates too expensive a minute ago, sir,' said the strange man. 'A pound is all I require, thank you.'

'Well, thank *you*,' said Dad, paying him.

'Yes, thank you, thank you, thank you,' said Rose. 'You really do work like magic.'

'I'm not sure it's exactly magic, but like I said, I can liven things up,' said the strange man.

'Well, you've livened things up for me all right,' said Rose, as she showed him to the door. 'It was so dead boring without the video.'

'I think life can be quite lively with or without a video,' said the strange man. 'You don't

want to waste all your time watching. You should be up and doing.'

'You're trying to liven *me* up now,' said Rose, laughing.

'That's right,' said the strange man, and he shook her hand.

Rose's entire arm tingled and her actual hand shone momentarily like a sparkler.

'Let's shake again,' said the strange man, and he took her left hand this time.

Rose's other arm tingled and her left hand lit up. She shivered with the shock. The strange man gave her one last flashing smile and stepped out of the door.

Rose was left in the dark hallway. She stared at her hands. They still glowed faintly in the gloom. She wriggled her fingers. Well, they still seemed to work all right. She tried shaking her own hands. There was no tingle at all. And the glow was going. She blinked. The glow was gone.

'Rose?' Dad called. He was still experimenting with the video, which was working perfectly.

'Isn't it great, Dad!' said Rose, doing a little lumbering dance around the living room.

'Well, yes, it's great — though I still don't get it,' said Dad, scratching his head. 'How

did he *do* it? Even if there was just some electrical short or something I still don't see how he could fix it with the tip of his finger like that. And look, see where Rick bodged it all up — it's all gone back neatly now.'

'He works-like-magic, Dad.'

'You're telling me. Well, let's celebrate, pal.' Dad dug into his trouser pockets. 'Nip down to Uncle Frank's and choose a video. Get some coke too, and I'll have crisps and you can have chocolate, whatever you want.'

'Oh Dad, thanks! Wow! Can I have two bars of chocolate, eh? And a packet of crisps too?'

Dad laughed. 'All right, but don't you dare tell your mum or you'll get me into trouble.' He handed Rose a five pound note. 'Get whatever you want out of that.'

'Whoopee,' Rose shouted and galloped out of the door.

'Better get something for Rick too,' Dad called after her.

Rose pondered this. Rick was busy rollerskating with his mates. She didn't really want to disturb him. He wouldn't want to come indoors and watch a video anyway. And he shouldn't eat while he was skating, he could easily choke himself. Rose decided to ignore her brother for his own good.

But Rick didn't ignore her. She did her new dance as she went under the arch of North block, skipping and flinging her arms about to express her happiness. Rick and Charlie suddenly shot past on their skates. They cracked up laughing, expressing their derision.

'Look at old Square-Bum!'

'She's waggling her square bum.'

'What's she doing, *dancing*?'

'Square-dancing!' Rick shouted, and they shrieked hysterically as they sped on their way.

Rose froze. She tingled with embarrassment. She wished she hadn't been daft enough to dance. If only Rick and Charlie hadn't seen her. They'd be teasing her about it for weeks now. She found she was clenching her left hand. It suddenly lit up and started glowing red, as if she'd just switched herself into action. And then astonishingly Rick and Charlie reappeared, skating backwards this time, so fast she could hardly see them. She was dancing again, her arms and legs whirring in the air, and then she was hurtling backwards into the lift and then running backwards along her own balcony.

'I'm rewinding!' said Rose, and she unclenched her left fist.

Immediately the world stopped whizzing backwards. Rose stood still. She looked at her left hand. She wiggled her fingers. They waved back at her merrily.

'Works-like-magic,' Rose whispered.

She could hear the whirr of the boys' wheels in the distance. In less than a minute they'd speed through the North block arch. But this time they weren't going to catch her dancing.

Rose got the lift downstairs and then nipped into the rubbish room and snaffled a couple of cardboard boxes. She ran with the boxes to the arch and then spread them across the road. Then she stood to attention, waiting.

Rick and Charlie came speeding round the bend towards the arch. They saw Rose. They saw the cardboard boxes. They tried to stop, but they were on a slope. They couldn't even slow down.

There was a crash. There was a bump and a bash and a bonk. There were yells. There were moans and whimpers. There were curses.

'Looks like you need to practise, boys. Not very steady on your skates yet, are you?' Rose jeered.

She walked off with her head in the air, waggling her fingers at them derisively.

4...

Rose selected *Lady and the Tramp* from Uncle Frank's. Dad didn't mind baby films a bit.

'So your video's working again? Great. That old chap fixed it without too much bother, did he?' said Uncle Frank.

'No bother at all,' said Rose, happily choosing chocolate. And crisps and coke. And more chocolate. And she didn't want to lumber Dad with a lot of loose change so she might just as well use up the rest on a Mars ice cream from Uncle Frank's fridge.

She didn't want the ice cream to melt so she leant on the wall outside Uncle Frank's, her carrier full of goodies on one arm, and got started on her ice cream. She sucked at the chocolate, making happy little slavery noises. She sounded like Robbie with his bottle but she didn't care. She bit into the sweet cold ice cream and shuddered with pleasure. She licked and sucked and bit until it was all gone. She wiped her tongue round the last little smear of chocolate inside the wrapper and sighed.

'I wish I had another,' Rose murmured.

And then she looked down at her sticky left hand. She smiled.

She clenched her left fist very slowly and the wrapper opened itself up and filled with chocolate ice cream. She kept her fist clenched a fraction too long and found herself stepping backwards into Uncle Frank's, chosing chocolate bars. It was a very pleasant spot to stop.

'So your video's working again? Great. That old chap fixed it without too much bother, did he?' said Uncle Frank, completely unaware that he was repeating himself.

Rose enjoyed the replay enormously. She went outside Uncle Frank's with her brand new Mars ice cream, leant against the wall, and ate it all up with immense enjoyment. She was almost full now but she decided it might be fun to see if her left hand was still in proper working order. So she clenched it again, quickly this time, so she whizzed backwards in one quick blink. She waggled her fingers and there she was choosing chocolates all over again.

'So your video's working again?' Uncle Frank started.

'Yes, it's great. That old chap fixed it without too much bother, yes he did,' Rose gabbled quickly.

Uncle Frank looked a bit taken aback. 'You took the words right out of my mouth.'

'Yes, I know,' Rose giggled, selecting her third Mars ice cream.

This third one took quite a lot of licking. Rose had to have a little rest when she was halfway through. But she was a determined girl and she certainly wasn't going to waste it. Rick came limping along as she took the last bit.

'You put those cardboard boxes in our way, didn't you! I'm going to get you for that, Square-Bum. And what's that you're eating, you greedy pig? A Mars ice cream! That's not fair, where's mine, eh?'

Rose licked the last wrapper thoughtfully. She'd got her own back on Rick but it might not be prudent to make him her Deadly Enemy Number One. She was nearly as big as Rick and if they had a fight she was quite good at squashing him, but Rick could devise all sorts of mean tortures like most big brothers.

'You want a Mars ice cream, do you, Rick?' Rose said sweetly. 'Just wait a sec.' She put her hand in her carrrier bag, clenching her left fist.

She flipped herself back into Uncle Frank's. It was almost starting to get boring. She let Uncle Frank say his little video-working-great-chap-fix-it speech and she selected the chocolate bars and the Mars ice cream. She went outside Uncle Frank's shop and opened up the ice cream wrapper. She took just one small cat-lick. She was starting to feel a little bit queasy. She waited. Rick came limping along. He started shouting angrily about cardboard boxes and Mars ice creams.

'That's not fair, where's mine, eh?'

'Here, Rick,' said Rose, holding out her almost untouched ice cream. 'You can have this one.'

Rick looked astonished.

'Why? What's the matter with it? You haven't dropped it in doggy's whoopsies, have you?'

'Don't be disgusting, Rick,' said Rose primly. 'This is a totally unsullied ice cream.' She

took a very tiny bite just to show him she hadn't poisoned it. Then she held the rest out to him. 'Go on, you have it.'

Rick took the ice cream and licked at it tentatively.

'Yes, it's great,' he said. 'So why don't you want it, eh?'

'I did. But I felt sorry for you, what with falling over again. Oh no, you haven't ripped your other jeans now, have you?'

'Maybe Mum won't notice,' said Rick, with touching optimism. He took a big bite of ice cream. 'Well. Thanks, Rose. That's really nice of you.'

Charlie staggered into view, his snub nose bleeding.

'You watch it, Square-Bum,' he shouted.

Rick frowned. He took another bite of ice cream. He sucked thoughtfully.

'Don't you call my sister Square-Bum,' he said. 'Or else I'll duff you up, see?'

Charlie blinked, looking surprised.

'But that's what you call her, Rick.'

'Yes, I know,' said Rick, munching Mars chocolate. 'But I'm her brother. You're not.'

There was no answer to that. Rose skipped back to the flat. She felt like doing her funny dance again but that might be asking for trouble.

Rose and Dad spent a very happy afternoon watching *Lady and the Tramp* and tucking into all the goodies from Uncle Frank's. Rose's appetite quickly returned. In fact she rewound herself and ate each chocolate bar twice. Dad unwittingly ate many packets of crisps and drank copious cans of coke but he didn't seem to mind. He enjoyed *Lady and the Tramp* just as much as Rose did.

'I saw it when I was a little kid. I've always loved it. Especially that bit where Lady and Tramp eat the plate of spaghetti,' Dad said, smiling.

'I'll rewind that bit for you then, Dad,' said Rose.

'No! You leave that video alone. Your mum was right, it was you eternally monkeying around with the video that made it pack up before. Now it's fixed — and I still can't work out what that old chap did, but never mind — I want it to *stay* fixed.'

'Yes, Dad.'

'You're not to touch the rewind or fast forward button, do you hear me?' said Dad.

'I hear and I obey, Great Masterful One,' said Rose. She didn't need to press the ordinary old rewind button on the video recorder any more. She could press her very own rewind and replay time itself. She clenched her fist until she got to the bit watching *Lady and the Tramp* where Dad started chuckling fondly at the spaghetti scene and then replayed it for his benefit — though he didn't know anything about it, of course.

At the end of the film Dad stretched and sighed. He looked at his watch.

'Gosh, I'd lost all track of time.'

'So did I, Dad,' said Rose.

'We'd better start getting tea ready for when Mum gets back,' said Dad. 'Maybe I shouldn't have eaten those crisps. I don't feel a bit hungry now. Funny that. I only ate one measly little packet and yet it feels like I've eaten six.'

'I wonder why,' said Rose innocently.

She was feeling pretty stuffed herself, and left half her baked potato at teatime.

'That's not like you, Rose,' said Mum. 'I think you must be sickening for something.'

'No I'm not. I'm just eating carefully. I'm trying to stick to a diet,' said Rose. It wasn't really a fib. She was taking extreme care to stick to a diet of chocolate and sweets and crisps and coke.

'Well, that's sensible, Rose, because you really are getting awfully podgy,' said Mum.

'Not to say square,' said Rick.

Rose looked at him reproachfully.

'I said *not* to say square. And I'm not going to,' said Rick.

'Just as well, brother dear,' said Rose. 'Or else I might start talking about jeans and rips and roller-skates.'

'Oh no Rick, not again!' said Mum.

'You rotten sneaky Square-Bum!' Rick bellowed. 'Tell tale tit.'

'No I'm not,' said Rose, but she wriggled uncomfortably. Maybe she wished she hadn't told now. It had been quite a novelty being on friendly terms with Rick. Now he was angrier than ever and it might not be to her advantage.

Well, she could change that. She clenched her left fist for a moment. Time rattled back a few seconds, to the square conversation. Rose opened up her hand and started again.

'Just as well you didn't say square, brother dear,' she said, but this time she snapped her mouth shut and wouldn't let the rip and roller-skates part out.

Rick gave her a little nod and a wink, and when Mum said it was Rose's turn to do the washing-up Rick started piling up the dishes too.

'I'll help you, unsquare sister,' he said.

'What's been going on this afternoon?' said Mum, unhooking a very sticky Robbie from his highchair and taking him off for his bath. 'I thought it seemed a bit weird that you somehow managed to get the video mended for only a pound, but now you two are being so nice to each other I know it's magic!'

'Works-like-magic,' Rose whispered happily, hugging herself.

'I wish there was some way of magicking all these dishes done,' said Rick, beginning to wish he hadn't been quite so obliging. 'We've got the gungy old baking tin to do as well. And all Robbie's gummed up baby dishes. We'll be *ages*.'

'We'll have to try to speed things up a little,' said Rose. She was looking at her hand. Not her left hand this time. The right one. She clenched her fist and it glowed, sending sparks right up her arm. And then she was suddenly jolted into action, flinging dishes in the sink, scrubbing at them in a fury, while Rick dried with dazzling speed and charged round the kitchen as if he were still wearing his roller-skates.

'We're fast-forwarding!' said Rose, and in two tiny seconds all the washing-up was done.

5...

Rose could barely get the waistband of her school skirt done up on Monday morning. She had a double-decker chocolate spread sandwich for breakfast and then rewound for a few minutes and ate it all over again. The quadruple sandwich was the last crumb. The button on the waistband fell off and the zip shot open.

'Mum, have you got a safety pin?' asked Rose.

'You kids,' said Mum, who'd spent over an hour last night sewing up half her son's garments. 'Come here, then. I'll sew the button on, I'm not having you wandering about with safety pins like a little punk. Well, breathe in, then, Rose, so I can see what I'm doing.'

'I *am* breathing in,' Rose gasped, with Mum down on her knees tugging at her skirt. 'Ouch! That was me,' she complained bitterly, as Mum started sewing up her waist rather than her waistband.

47

'Well, honestly. You're getting so big. I thought you were supposed to be on a diet,' said Mum. 'You ought to try to eat more sensibly, love. No more chocolate. You should eat salads, boiled fish, cottage cheese -'

'Salads are stupid, boiled fish is boring, cottage cheese is crummy,' Rose gabbled.

She was starting to find the whole conversation stupid and boring and crummy so she clenched her right fist. The button was sewn on in a trice, Mum changed Robbie's nappy with one flick of the wrist, and they were all off and out the door in a blink. Rose unclenched her fist, not wanting to get to school too quickly.

She was walking along the road with Rick, who was teetering on his roller-skates.

'Funny,' said Rick, shaking his head and looking dazed. 'I seem to have got ready in a bit of a rush. One minute you'd bust your button and Mum was nagging on at you for being fat and then the next ... we're here.'

'I'm not fat. I'm just big,' said Rose. She glared at Rick who was a very thin and wiry boy. 'I'd much sooner be big than a skinny spider like you.'

'You ought to take more exercise, then you'd get skinny too,' said Rick relentlessly. 'I'll hire you out my roller-skates if you like. Ten pence for ten minutes, how about it?'

'Get knotted,' said Rose. 'I don't want to borrow your stupid old skates. I can go as fast as I want just with my own feet.'

'You what? Did you say you can go *fast*? Hang on a minute, are you the same sister who came last in the running race *and* the skipping race and even the egg and spoon race on Sports Day?'

'You shut up. I didn't want to be bothered with those dopey races. But I can run really really fast if I want,' said Rose. 'I'll show you.' It wouldn't work if Rick raced along beside her while she fast-forwarded. He'd go quicker too and beat her by miles. 'You stand still and just watch, OK?' said Rose.

Rick folded his arms and leant against a lamp post, sniggering.

'Right,' said Rose, and clenched her right fist. She hurtled forwards, practically flying through the air. She was down outside the school before she could stop herself. She opened her hand out and waved triumphantly at Rick, who was now a tiny matchstick boy in the distance.

'See!' Rose bellowed.

Rick had certainly seen. He came roller-skating up to her, looking utterly bewildered.

'I told you,' said Rose, and swanned into school triumphantly.

Her cheeriness chilled a little as she went into her classroom. She wasn't enjoying school very much nowadays. She had a horrible strict teacher called Mrs Mackay who kept clapping her hands and saying 'That's quite enough, Rose. Now just sit down and stop showing off.' Mrs Mackay didn't let them talk much in class, and they had to do proper lessons like Arithmetic and English. Mrs Mackay even spoilt the fun lessons like Art and Music and Movement. Rose wasn't allowed to paint lovely sploshy pictures of flying elephants and wicked witches. She had to paint incredibly boring things like *A Spring Day* or *An Autumn Wood*, and Mrs Mackay nagged if she went over the lines. Rose couldn't make up her own swirly swooshy dances in Music and Movement. Mrs Mackay wanted them to learn special steps and the boys could march but the girls had to be on their tippy-toes. Rose snorted in disgust.

'Good morning, Rose,' said Mrs Mackay, eyebrows raised. 'Are you doing a pig impersonation?'

The children giggled and Rose burned.

'No Mrs Mackay,' she mumbled.

'Then stop that silly snorting, please. Now sit down and get out your Arithmetic book.'

Rose sighed deeply. She looked at her hands. Maybe she could fast forward herself through lessons to playtime? But then it was PE and now they were in Mrs Mackay's class they had to play Rounders, and Rose could never hit the silly ball or catch it either come to that. She'd have to fast forward PE too. In fact if she didn't watch out she'd be fast forwarding steadily right though the Juniors and she'd be at Secondary School before it was time to go home.

Rose wasn't too sure about Secondary School. Some of the boys in Rick's gang were already at the Comprehensive and they kept telling horrible tales about your lunch being nicked by other kids and if you made a fuss

you got beaten up in the toilets. Rose wasn't convinced they were telling the truth but she wasn't terribly keen to find out one way or another. Changing schools was certainly going to be a big step. Going up into the Juniors from the Infants school had just been a little hop.

Rose had loved life in the Infants, especially the first baby class. There were no proper lessons and you could talk all you wanted. She'd had a lovely teacher called Miss Flower who'd made a special fuss of Rose because she had a flowery name too. Miss Flower pinned Rose's paintings up on the wall. Miss Flower asked Rose to sing a song because she had a good loud voice. Miss Flower laughed and clapped when Rose made up a little dance to make listening to the song more interesting. Miss Flower *never* said 'That's quite enough, Rose. Now just sit down and stop showing off.'

I wish I was back in the Infants, Rose thought.

Then she thought some more. She looked at her left hand. She wondered if there was some way of locking it into position so she could whizz back into the past in a matter of seconds. Her hand started glowing at the thought. Of its own accord her thumb tucked in tight and she had an overwhelming urge to press it hard. It looked like she'd worked out the way.

But what if it didn't work properly? What if she zapped herself too far back? She really didn't fancy being a baby again, wearing soggy nappies and only able to say goo-goo gargle-gargle like baby Robbie. You couldn't have a snack whenever you got peckish, you had to yell your head off until Mum got the message and stuck a bottle in your mouth. And even if you got fat from all the feeds you were still little. It was a long time before Rose got big enough to hold her own against Rick. In fact it was sometimes still a struggle nowadays. Maybe it would be better to stay firmly in the present?

'Now, we're going to do some Problems in Arithmetic today,' said Mrs Mackay. 'Rose, come up to the blackboard.'

Rose had a serious problem tackling Problems. If it took six men three hours to dig a hole in a field it took one girl half a second to clench her fist tightly over her thumb and whizz herself back to the past.

'W-h-e-e-e-e-e-e,' Rose squeaked, as she went whirling backwards, so fast this time that she couldn't possibly keep track, she couldn't stop, she couldn't change her mind, she couldn't even think, she just unspooled through her past life until suddenly her thumb shot out of her fist, her hand opened and she was shaken right back into her five year old self.

'What's the matter, Rose?' said a gentle voice, and a sweetly familiar figure in a soft blue frock bent down by the tiny chair.

'It really is you, Miss Flower!' said Rose. She looked down at herself and saw her own

soppy little checked frock and her long-ago red shoes with straps and when she shook her head she felt the two wispy plaits she'd once worn bounce about on her shoulders.

'Of course, it's me,' said Miss Flower. 'I think you must have fallen asleep for a minute, Rose! Wake up now, poppet.'

Rose was wide awake now and raring to go.

'I'm really in the Infants class,' she said, looking round the bright friendly room with the finger-painting easels and the water trough and the playhouse in the corner and the pink dough — oh, she'd forgotten all about the pleasures of playing with pink dough!

She settled herself at the dough table and stuck her fingers into the lovely squashy ball of dough. Her fingers were small and fat and five years old, but her mind was still her own and had sophisticated ideas. She wasn't going to make boring old sausages or snakes or necklaces like the other children. She stroked the pink dough, sniffing its strange smell. She decided to model a rose. Yes, a beautiful pink rose, with a tight bud and curling petals. She could feel it blooming beneath her fingers.

She set to work fashioning a petal. But her hands were hopelessly clumsy now. When she tried to roll the dough into thin strips her fingers bunched and botched. When she tried to curl the edge of a petal it broke off completely. When she tried to stick several petals together she pressed too hard and the rose got squashed into a shapeless lump.

Rose groaned, despairing. She found she had baby tears in her eyes.

'What's the matter, Rose?' asked Miss Flower.

'I can't make the dough work,' said Rose, sniffing and snorting.

'Yes, you can, dear. Why, that's lovely! A dear little pig.'

A pig, indeed! She couldn't seem to get away from pigs today.

'How about doing some finger painting now?' Miss Flower suggested tactfully, as Rose crossly flattened the pig-rose into a pancake.

Rose pulled on an apron, fiddling with the fasteners for ages before they would pop into place. She stood at the easel, dipped a finger into the pot of paint, and started on a self portrait. She wanted to paint her plaits with ribbons and her check frock and her red shoes with straps. But her finger wouldn't paint what she wanted. It drew a stupid round

shape with spidery arms and legs. It didn't even manage a head, let alone hair. It smeared two blobby eyes right in the middle of the chest, and a smiley mouth straight across the stomach.

Rose stamped her red shoes.

'What's the matter, Rose?' said Miss Flower yet again.

'I can't make the paint work either,' Rose moaned.

'Oh dear, you are having trouble today,' said Miss Flower. She came and looked at Rose's picture. 'But it's a beautiful painting, you funny girl.'

'What is it?' said Rose. She peered up at Miss Flower.

Miss Flower hesitated. She looked at the painting intently.

'It's not another pig,' said Rose.

'Of course it's not,' Miss Flower agreed. 'It's a picture of you.' It was probably just a lucky guess.

'It's a picture of me looking like a pig,' said Rose, and she couldn't feel proud when Miss Flower pinned the silly painting on the wall.

Perhaps it wasn't such fun being an Infant again after all. Rose's hands were so helpless. She didn't have much luck weaving a little raffia mat and though she could manage to thread big beads onto a piece of string it soon became terribly boring. She tried chatting to the other children in her class, but they just prattled on about baby things.

Rose brightened when Miss Flower clapped her hands and told them to sit in a circle because it was story time. Rose recognised the little girl and boy on the cover of the book.

'Oh, it's Topsy and Tim. I remember! I read that ages and ages ago,' Rose said.

'Did you, Rose?' said Miss Flower. Her eyebrows were raised and her blue eyes were twinkling. She obviously thought Rose was telling stories herself.

'I did, really I did. I read all the Topsy and Tim books,' Rose insisted.

'Well. I expect you've looked at the pictures,' said Miss Flower.

'No, I can read! It's easy-peasy,' said Rose, and she went and stood next to Miss Flower, looking at the book on her lap.

She'd show her. She'd read it right through to the whole class. She might be back in her five year old body but she could still remember how to read, for goodness sake.

Or could she? She looked at the squiggly black shapes on the page. She could pick out an 'a' here, an 'e' there ...but that was all! She looked at a big letter that might be a 'T' but she didn't even know whether it was T for Topsy or T for Tim. She felt so silly standing there in front of the whole class. She clenched her fat little fists. She was tired of being little and stupid. She tucked her right thumb tight

inside her fist. The circle of children seemed to start spinning. Miss Flower's kind face faded. Rose suddenly rushed forwards, hurtling through time, round and round so quickly that when she suddenly stopped with a jerk and found herself standing at the blackboard feeling silly all over again she staggered and nearly fell, the chalk in her hand squeaking all the way down the board.

Mrs Mackay thought she'd fainted. Rose was hurried off to the school sickroom. The secretary tucked her up on the sofa and gave her a cup of sweet tea and a digestive biscuit. Rose managed to miss the entire arithmetic lesson after all. This Little Piggy Rose went hee-hee-hee all the way home.

6...

Rose kept looking at her hands as she walked towards her block of flats. If her left hand could rewind her years back into the past then perhaps her right hand could hurtle her years into the future? She kept opening and closing her fingers, waggling them about, wondering.

Rick and his mate Charlie passed her on their roller-skates. Charlie waggled his fingers back at her.

'Hi there, Square-Bum,' he shouted.

Rose was too preoccupied to do more than toss her head at him. She had to sort this out carefully. It was a bit scary thinking of zapping straight into the future. At least she knew what had happened in the past. Suppose there was some terrible war or disaster in ten years' time and she ended up right in the middle of it? And what if she got stuck and couldn't get back? The video had broken down, after all. What if Rose's fist suddenly went phut and stopped working too?

'Hello, Rose,' said Cherry Chalmers, who lived along the balcony. 'Do you want to come and play with me?'

Rose hesitated. Cherry was only six and she was a right pain. She had long fair hair that her Mum did up in ringlets and great big brown eyes like Bambi and when she was three she'd been a runner-up in the Miss Pears contest. Her Mum had all the photos up on the wall, hundreds of glossy pictures of Cherry in a pink party frock, and Cherry's best French doll had a special pink party frock to match.

Cherry was the sort of child Rose avoided like the plague *but* she was allowed to help herself to as many ice lollies from the fridge as she wanted and her Mum usually had a big box of chocolates on the go and handed them around quite often.

'We can watch videos if you want,' said Cherry.

Rose decided to take a little break from time-travelling and had a relaxing afternoon watching *Alice in Wonderland* and sucking first a raspberry ice lolly, then an orange one, and finally a lime lolly.

'My insides must look like a traffic light,' said Rose.

'Do you want to try one of my Belgian fresh cream chocolates, dear?' said Cherry's mum.

'Mmm, yes please,' said Rose.

Cherry's mum was very kind and kept handing round her chocolates. Rose started to feel a bit of a greedy pig after she'd eaten five on the trot but her mouth still watered when she looked at the box. She solved things by gently clenching her left hand and rewinding a few minutes so she could accept the last especially wonderful chocolate cream all over again — and again and again.

She found she lost track of real time and Rick had to come knocking on the door to fetch her.

'Hello Rick,' said Cherry enthusiastically, tossing her long curls. 'Have you come to play too?'

'I don't play with little girls,' said Rick, looking mortally offended. 'I've come to get Rose. Mum's back and she's getting tea.'

'Is it teatime already?' said Rose, who didn't feel quite ready for tea now.

She thanked Cherry and her Mum for having her and went along the balcony to her own flat to tackle spaghetti bolognaise.

'Like in *Lady and the Tramp*, eh, Dad?' said Rose, valiantly doing her best to stuff long strands of spaghetti into her mouth.

Rick was sucking his spaghetti up very noisily, strand by strand.

'Rick! Behave yourself,' said Mum, chopping up Robbie's tiny portion.

Rose decided to compete. She sucked her own spaghetti, making wonderful slurping sounds.

'Rose! Now stop it, both of you,' Mum snapped. 'You kids don't half get on my nerves sometimes.'

Robbie decided Rick and Rose were getting too much attention. He leant forward in his high chair, grabbed his dish and sank his head right into the spaghetti.

'Robbie!' Mum shrieked.

Robbie bobbed up again, snorting with laughter, his face bright orange, little strands of spaghetti sticking to his eyelashes. He looked so comical that Rose and Rick dissolved into helpless laughter, and even Dad had a bit of a splutter to himself.

Mum wasn't at all amused.

'Don't laugh at him, it'll only make him worse. He'll start doing it at every meal —

and then I'm the poor Mrs Twerpy who has to mop him up.'

'Well, you shouldn't have had another baby, Mum,' said Rose unwisely.

'I shouldn't have had any of you,' said Mum darkly. 'I can't wait for the three of you to be grown-up and off my hands, I'm telling you.'

'We'll live it up a bit then, eh?' said Dad. 'I'll be done with night shifts then, so we can go out and enjoy ourselves in the evenings.'

'Yes, you kids will be the ones stuck in with yelling babies,' said Mum, unstrapping a struggling Robbie, who did his best to rub spaghetti in her hair and an orange swirly pattern all down her jumper.

'Who, me?' said Rick. 'I'm never going to have kids. The King of the Rollerball doesn't have *kids*.'

'You wait and see. I thought I was going to be playing Centre Forward for England — and now look at me,' said Dad, sighing. 'We don't know what the future holds in store for us.'

'I could find out,' said Rose, and she suddenly decided to give it a go. She looked down at her hands under the table. Her right hand was glowing like a little electric fire. She

71

tucked her thumb right into her palm and squeezed it tightly, making a hard fist.

She was suddenly jolted forward, swooping through the table, through the flat, through time itself. She tried to keep her eyes open to see if she could make sense of what was happening, but there was a great howling wind that made her eyes stream.

'I want to go right into the future, to when we're all grown up,' Rose cried out above the high-pitched roaring in her ears.

She had no idea whether she was going to make it safely. She seemed to be hurtling on

forever. What if she carried on until she was an old lady and died? How could she ever get back then? She tried to open up her right hand but her arms flailed helplessly in the air, out of her control.

Then the roaring and the whirling got louder and wilder and she was suddenly jolted into place so violently that she shook all over.

'Rose? Are you all right? You didn't get a shock from that cable, did you? Here, you'd better sit down.'

Rose opened her eyes and blinked. She was in a strange large room with cameras and cables all over the place. There were very bright lights right in front of her and several people in odd clothes and a lot of make-up were standing in front of half a kitchen.

Rose blinked again. Did they only have rooms with three walls in the future? And why was the lighting so strange, was there something wrong with everyone's eyes? And what about all these cameras ...?

She suddenly understood. This wasn't her home. She was at work in a film studio. All the people on the set were looking at her, obviously waiting for her to tell them what to do.

She swivelled in her seat and looked at the back of her canvas chair. There was one word spelled out in big letters. DIRECTOR. Oh boy! *She was directing her own video!*

'I'm fine, folks,' she said jumping up and into action.

She found she knew what she was doing. She bossed the actors around quite a lot but they didn't seem to mind at all. Then she decided they all needed a break and someone went running for coffee and sandwiches. Rose had a sticky bun and a bar of chocolate too. She was the director. She didn't have to fuss about staying skinny like the actresses. Maybe it was just as well.

She was very curious when it was time to go home because she didn't have a clue where her home would be. She found there was someone waiting for her outside the studio.

'There you are, Rosie. I've been waiting for you for ages. Oh darling, I'm going crazy without you. Please come back to me. We'll get married if that's what you want,' this total stranger declared, throwing his arms round her.

Rose blinked up at him. He was fair and freckled, and he might have been good look-

ing if he didn't have such a snub nose. There was something strangely familiar about that funny nose.

'It's Charlie!' said Rose, and she burst out laughing.

Charlie got very annoyed with her for laughing at him. It took her ages to calm him, and he wouldn't understand that she wasn't ready to be tied down.

'I don't see why you're so dead set against marriage. Rick's happy enough,' said Charlie.

'Rick's married?' giggled Rose.

Charlie looked at her strangely.

'Let's go and visit him,' said Rose, not wanting to miss this for the world.

It turned out Rick and Cherry and their three children lived in a maisonette on the same estate as Rose's mum and dad. Yes, *Cherry*. There aren't many Cherrys bobbing about, and the moment Rose saw the long blonde curls and big Bambi eyes she knew that Rick really had married her. And he looked so happy too, making the supper and chatting to his children while Cherry kicked off her high heels and lounged on the sofa, exhausted after a hard day at the office.

'I never thought I'd see you doing the cooking, Rick,' said Rose.

'Well, I'm not a patch on our Robbie,' said Rick. 'Did Mum tell you? He came top on his fancy cookery course and now this posh Italian restaurant's offered him a job.'

'Little Robbie!' Rose gasped. 'I want to go and see him, and Mum and Dad.'

Charlie stayed behind to have a go at fixing the family car, which had been in a series of minor accidents. Rick didn't seem any more skilled on four wheels than he was on his roller-skates.

Rose went into her own block of flats, reassured to see they looked much the same as ever. Her front door was even still painted the same colour. It was a shock when an old man opened the door to her.

'Dad?' said Rose.

'Hello, Rosy-Posy! What a lovely surprise. Your mum will be thrilled. Come on in then, love.'

'Are you all right, Dad?' Rose asked anxiously. 'You look so ... tired.'

Dad laughed and told her not to be so cheeky. He looked more like the real Dad when he laughed, and Rose relaxed.

'Hi, Sis,' said a handsome hulking great boy who towered over her. 'I've got some of my special cassata ice cream in the fridge, do you want to try some?'

'You bet!' said Rose, immensely pleased with the way her little brother had turned out.

But when she saw Mum she wavered. Mum was an old lady, even more lined than Dad, and when she tried to get out her chair to welcome Rose she winced a little, rubbing her hip.

'Mum, what is it?' Rose cried, alarmed.

'Just my arthritis, love, that's all. Oh Rose, this is a treat! You're such a naughty girl, you never come home enough. Come and give your old mum a hug.'

Rose hurried to hug Mum. She realised that she was taller now. Mum felt so little and frail in her arms. Rose felt she might burst into tears.

'Oh Mum, I think I've grown up too quickly,' said Rose, and as she hugged Mum tighter she found herself clenching her left hand, her thumb tucked in tight.

Then her arms were empty, and she was whirling backwards through time, tumbling helplessly until suddenly her fingers opened and there she was, back in her old young self.

'Rose?' said Dad. 'What's up? You seemed to go off in a little daydream just then.'

'That's right,' said Rose shakily. 'Dreaming about the future. Oh Dad, you do look nice and *young*.'

'Well, thanks dear,' said Dad, flexing his muscles.

'I bet *I* look a hundred. I certainly feel it,' Mum moaned, still struggling with the spaghetti-strewn Robbie.

'No you don't, Mum, you look lovely,' said Rose. 'Here, let me take Robbie, he's too heavy for you.'

'Don't be daft,' said Mum. 'You don't want your clothes mucked up too.' She held Robbie at arms' length. 'Look what you've done to my good jumper, you little monster.'

'Don't get cross with him, Mum, he's only practising. He's going to develop a feel for Italian food,' said Rose.

'Oh yes? And how would you know?' said Mum.

'You'd be surprised,' said Rose.

She clasped her hands and they gave off little sparks. She still hadn't found out where she lived in the future. She could try again tomorrow. She had lots of tomorrows. And some yesterdays. But right now she was a bit tired of time-travelling and wanted to stick in today.

She bathed Robbie for Mum and then cleared up all the tea things, and Mum was so grateful she gave her two pounds for another video.

Rose danced off down to Uncle Frank's.

'Get that wiggle, Square-Bum!' Charlie shouted down from the balcony.

Rose tossed her head.

'Turns you on, does it, Charlie?' she shouted back.

She leapt and twirled and twiddled her feet, snapping her sparkly fingers. Charlie blinked down at her, his mouth open.

There was a sudden crackle behind her. Rose whirled round, and there was the strange old man in his raincoat smiling at her, teeth flashing.

'You're looking lively now, little lady,' he said, clapping her dance.

The air sizzled as his hands met.

'I've been up and doing *ever* such a lot,' said Rose breathlessly.

'I'm glad to hear it. Your video's still working, I take it?'

'Oh yes, it's working beautifully. And so am I,' said Rose. 'We both work like magic now.'

There was a sudden ringing noise like a telephone.

'Hello? WORKS-LIKE-MAGIC. How can I help you?' said the old man.

There was a buzzy sound of someone speaking on the telephone. Only there wasn't any sign of a telephone, not even the sleekest new portable model.

'I'm sure I can fix your video,' said the old man. 'I'll be right with you, in two shakes of a lamb's tail.'

He winked at Rose, and then suddenly disappeared in a blue flash, raincoat flapping.

Rose waved at the empty space.

'What's going on, Square-Bum?' Charlie hissed, his eyes boggling.

Rose snapped her fingers at him dismissively, and sauntered off to the video shop.

'Hello there, Video Rose,' said Uncle Frank.

It seemed a good nickname. It was certainly better than Square-Bum.

Yes. Video Rose.

MARK SPARK

"*Mark Spark!*" said Miss Moss.
"Give some of the others a chance to
answer, please."
Mark slumped in his seat. He
wasn't impressed.

Chapter One

"Hands up all of you with a dog at home," said Miss Moss.

Mark's friend Jason put his hand up. Jason had a spaniel called Ben who had once eaten a whole box of chocolates in ten minutes flat. Louise from down the road had her hand up. Louise had a poodle called Puffball who whined a lot. Mark felt he would whine too if he had to wear a red ribbon and a silly tartan coat. That was no way to treat a dog. It wasn't fair. Mark would have loved a dog but he couldn't have one.

Mark's mum and dad were out at work all day so there would be no one to look after a dog. There was no one to look after Mark when he came home from school so Mark always went round to Great Gran's for his tea. Then he got another tea when Mum came to fetch him home. Mark was very nearly as greedy as Jason's spaniel Ben.

"Tell me all the different things your dogs can do," said Miss Moss.

"Jason's dog can eat heaps," said Mark. "And then he's sick heaps too."

"Mark Spark!" (He was really called Mark Spencer, but everyone

called him Mark Spark. Even Miss Moss).

"And Louise's dog whines and whimpers like this," said Mark, imitating Puffball.

"*Mark Spark!*" said Miss Moss. "Give some of the others a chance to answer, please."

Mark slumped in his seat. He listened to the other children telling long stories about Woofer and Bruce and Rover. He wasn't impressed.

"So your dogs can fetch their own leads and open doors and bark at strangers. But I'm going to show you a picture of a very clever dog who can do something else. Something very important indeed," said Miss Moss.

Mark looked at the big picture
Miss Moss was holding. He saw a
cream labrador in a special harness
leading a woman with dark glasses.

"This lady's blind. She can't see at
all. Try closing your eyes for a
moment. Now imagine you've got to

get yourself out of the classroom, across the playground, out of the gate and all the way home without once opening your eyes. It would be very difficult, wouldn't it?"

Mark's eyes were open, not shut. He had his hand up and was bouncing around in his seat.

"I know what it's like, Miss. My
Great Gran's blind. She can't go out,
well, not much."

"Don't shout, Mark. It can't be
easy to be your Great Granny. Now,
this dog is a specially trained guide
dog. He's leading the lady along,
helping her safely across the road.

Guide dogs like this one do a wonderful job. But it takes lots of money to train them. Our school is going to try to raise enough money to train a special guide dog. Now, how can our class make some money?"

"I've got an idea, Miss," said Mark.

"Let's hear from someone else for a change," said Miss Moss. "Louise?"

"We could have a bring and buy sale, Miss Moss," said Louise. She liked bringing and was very good at buying.

"We could have a sponsored run," said Jason, who always came first at running.

"I've got a better idea," said

Mark, who simply couldn't keep quiet. "Let's have a parade with all of us dressed up as guide dogs with collecting tins round our necks and we could have my Great Gran at the back of the parade and we could be leading her. We could all go *woof*, *woof*, *woof* and —"

"That's enough, Mark. It's certainly an original idea but I don't think it's very practical. Still, I'm glad you're showing such an interest."

Chapter Two

No wonder Mark was interested. He boasted to Jason and Louise all the way home.

"Just wait till you see my Great Gran out with her guide dog! He'll have to go very slowly so my Great Gran can keep up. I'll train him to be ever so careful."

"Don't talk daft, Mark Spark," said Louise. "They have proper trainers for the guide dogs."

"And Miss Moss didn't say your

Great Gran was getting this guide dog," said Jason.

"She's blind so of course she'll get one," said Mark. "Wait till my Great Gran hears."

"I think the whole street can hear," said Jason, wincing away from Mark. "You don't half bellow sometimes, Mark."

Mark was used to talking in a loud voice for Great Gran because she was a little deaf as well as blind. She couldn't hear when Mark knocked at her door so he had his own key.

"*Great Gran!*" Mark yelled, flying through her hall.

Great Gran wasn't great at all. She was a very little lady and when Mark went bounding straight on top of her she nearly got squashed.

"What's this, the human whirlwind?" she said. "Get off of me, you great lump!" but she laughed and tickled Mark.

"D-o-o-o-n't!" Mark squealed. He was very ticklish, especially under the arms. "Give over, Great Gran. Listen!"

"I can't help but listen, Mr Squirm-and-Squiggle. You hungry? The teapot's brewing and there's marmite and crisp sandwiches and jammy buns."

"Wow, great. But do listen, Great Gran. You're going to get a dog!"

"No, I'm not!"

"Yes, you are. My school's saving up to get you a dog."

"What would I be doing with a dog at my age, you soppy date? I can't even get out myself, let alone take a dog for a walk."

"That's the point, Great Gran," said Mark, tucking into his tea. "You don't have to take the dog for a walk. It can take *you* for a walk. It's a guide

dog, get it?" Mark sprayed crisp crumbs in his excitement.

"Oh, one of them," said Great Gran. "Yes, they're a smashing idea. That young girlie I see up at the eye hospital, she's going to be getting a guide dog. It'll make all the difference to her. She'll be able to pop into the town or slip out of an evening no bother at all."

"But I want you to have a guide

dog, Great Gran!" said Mark, so
upset that he actually stopped eating.

"They'd never give me a guide
dog, pet. I'm too old. I couldn't get
out and about even if I had a dog.
And I'd have to be taught how to
look after it, and *I'm* too old a dog to
learn new tricks."

"Ooooh," said Mark, bitterly

disappointed. "Why do you have to be so old, Great Gran?"

"That's what I ask myself, little chum. Here, have a jammy bun. Have them both, darling, you're a growing boy."

Mark ate both buns and felt a bit better. They settled down in front of the television and watched *Neighbours* (Great Gran just listened) and then Mark read aloud. They were reading

from a big fat paperback called *Love's Flame*. They hadn't got to any flaming bits yet, but there was a lot of love. They were the bits Great Gran and Mark liked best. He read in funny voices, deep down in his tummy for Sir Jasper and high up and silly for Roseanne the servant girl. Great Gran laughed until her eyes went weepy. Mark laughed too and forgot about the guide dog.

Chapter Three

Mark still wanted to help raise the money for the guide dog all the same.

Miss Moss decided to try the Bring and Buy sale first.

"Bring lots of gifts," said Miss Moss.

Jason was bringing a big box of chocolates (if he could keep them out of Ben's way).

Louise was bringing a big plush teddy she'd never played with and some old videos and a knitted toilet roll cover made by her mum.

Mark had problems deciding what to bring. He wanted all his toys and his mum was too busy to make anything.

"I can knit," said Great Gran. "I'll knit you up a pair of socks quick as a wink."

"Thanks," said Mark doubtfully. Great Gran had never been much of a knitter even when she could see.

He felt even more doubtful when
she produced the socks. They were
made out of scraps of wool so they
didn't even match. One was mostly
pink, with yellow stripes. The other
was red with black at the top.

"Do they look all right?" said
Great Gran. "I think I might have
dropped a stitch or two."

"They look smashing," said Mark
loyally.

The other children didn't think
they looked smashing when he

slipped them on the Bring and Buy stall. They laughed and pointed.

"Whoever brought those awful old socks?" they said.

Jason knew. Louise knew. They looked at each other. They looked at Mark.

"I think they're absolutely brilliant socks," said Mark fiercely. "I've simply got to have them before anyone else snaps them up. Only thirty pence? That's a real bargain!"

He bought the socks himself. He put them on there and then, although they looked even odder on the leg. Mark only had five pence left to spend now. Nowhere near enough for the box of chocolates.

"Well, they'll keep your feet warm

anyway," said Jason.

"They look dead trendy," lied Louise.

Mark smiled at his friends and didn't mind quite so much about the chocolates. And at least Great Gran's

socks weren't left lying unwanted on
the stall. Louise's mum's knitted
toilet roll cover was reduced right
down to five pence and still no one
would buy it. Louise was getting very
pink in the face.

"I'll buy it as a present for my Great Gran," said Mark. "I bet she'll like it."

Great Gran liked it a lot.

"What a dear little knitted hat. I'll pop it on every time I go out in the back yard. It'll keep my head nice and cosy."

Great Gran's socks kept Mark's feet more than cosy. He wore them when they had their sponsored walk. (Miss Moss thought a run might prove too energetic).

The walk seemed energetic enough for Mark. Jason rushed ahead right away. Then Louise left Mark far behind. Soon Mark was trailing round the playing fields by himself.

He sat down for a little rest. He

took his shoes off and aired his molten feet. One toe had poked a little hole in the red sock already. It looked like a nose peeping through. Mark wiggled his toe and made the sock stick its nose in the air. Then he made the sock sneeze. He'd have liked to play socks for the rest of the afternoon but he had to put his shoes back on and crawl round the playing field again. And again. And again. And even then he didn't do anywhere near as many circuits as Louise, let alone Jason. Left to Mark, they wouldn't manage as much as a puppy paw or the tip of a tail.

Chapter Four

"What am I going to do, Great Gran?" said Mark, munching a condensed milk sandwich. "I've been useless at this fund-raising lark so far. And now Miss Moss says our class are going to give a concert, charging ten pence a seat."

"That'll be fun, lovie," said Great Gran.

"No, it won't," Mark wailed, not watching his sandwich carefully enough. Condensed milk dripped

down his wrist and up his shirt
sleeve, so he had to lick it quickly.
"I don't know what to do in this
concert, Great Gran. Jason's going to
sing a pop song but Miss Moss says
I've got a voice like a fog horn.
Louise is going to do a ballet dance

and she's wearing a special fairy costume but I can't dance for toffee."

"I can't see you being a fairy, pet," said Great Gran. "Can't you say a poem? You're ever so comic. You always have me in stitches when you read *Love's F. ne*."

Mark thought hard, sticking his finger into the jug of condensed milk and then licking it. He did a lot of sticking and licking. Sometimes it was just as well Great Gran couldn't see properly.

"Maybe we could act *Love's Flame*? I could get Louise to be Roseanne, only she'd try to do it properly and then it wouldn't be funny. Maybe Jason could be Roseanne? No, he'd feel soppy. *I'd* be Roseanne, only I've got to do Sir Jasper."

"Can't you do it all, pet? *I* know. Act it all out with puppets," said Great Gran.

"Yes! But how can I make
puppets? I'm not much good at Art
and Craft."

"You'll have to keep it simple.
Glove puppets."

"Glove puppets," said Mark, and
then he snapped his sticky fingers
and grinned. "I've got an idea."

The concert was a big success.
Jason sang his song. Louise did her
ballet dance. Some of the boys

whistled when they saw her pink
ballet frock and Louise went pink
too, but she got on with her dance
and didn't wobble once. Then she
gave a fancy curtsey while everyone
clapped.

But the Mark Spark Puppet Show was the smash hit of the concert. The puppet booth was a big cardboard box. Mark crouched down behind it and stuck his hands up over the top, working the two puppets. It made his arms ache but he carried on regardless. He spoke in Roseanne's high squeaky voice while he made the pink and yellow puppet prance. (He'd simply sewn two blue button eyes on the stripey sock and tied on a hankie as an apron.) Then he spoke in Sir Jasper's big booming voice and made the red and black puppet bounce about. (Two brown buttons for his eyes and Mark's finger poking through the hole made a perfect nose.) Mark changed some of the *Love's Flame* story, giving Sir Jasper a

terrible cold so that he could sneeze a
lot. He made the love scenes sillier
than ever, and every time the Sir
Jasper sock puppet pounced sneezily
on Roseanne, murmuring daft
endearments, the children roared
with laughter. Miss Moss looked a
little twitchy at first, but then she

started laughing too, and at the end
of Mark's performance she stood up
and cheered.

Mark had to act out the entire
puppet show at Great Gran's that
teatime, and she chuckled and clapped
and called him a proper caution, good
enough to go on the stage.

"That's what Miss Moss said,
Great Gran," said Mark. "And guess
what! She says I should do a puppet
show in the playground every day
and charge everyone a penny a time

to come and watch. I'm going to
raise pounds and pounds for the
guide dog."

Mark didn't quite raise pounds
and pounds, but he certainly raised
lots and lots of pennies. Eventually
there was enough money to train a
guide dog. The school was sent a big
coloured photo of this very special
dog. His name was printed at the

bottom. He wasn't called Woofer or Bruce or Rover. He wasn't called Ben. He certainly wasn't called Puffball.

He was called Mark.

MARK SPARK
IN THE DARK

Mark hurtled out of bed, out of the
bedroom, down the stairs three at a time,
down the passage and out the back door.
Into the dark. The great black terrifying
outdoor dark.

Chapter One

Mark Spark walked home from school with his friends Jason and Louise. It was raining hard. Jason was wearing his big black wellie boots. He stamped happily in every puddle. Louise was wearing her Kermit-the-frog wellie boots. She sloshed her way along the gutter, taking her twin Kermits for a paddle.

Mark Spark didn't have any wellie boots. Still, he didn't see why Jason and Louise should have all the fun.

He took a running jump at every puddle and landed with a big splash. He waded through the stream in the gutter and dabbled about in the sludge blocking the drains. His socks were soon sodden and his new trainers started to squelch.

"Your mum's going to get mad when she sees those trainers. You only had them on your birthday, didn't you?" said Jason.

"Mmm," said Mark, looking at his new trainers. They didn't look very new now. Jason was right. Mark's mum was going to get mad.

"I'm not frightened of my mum," said Mark, jumping in another puddle. He always had his tea with Great Gran, before Mum got back

from work. Maybe Great Gran could cook his trainers as well as his tea so they'd be dry by the time Mum saw them?

"I'm getting new trainers for my birthday too," said Louise. "Pink, to match my pink T-shirt and my pink leggings. Mark, come out of that puddle. Yuck, it's all gungy!"

Some of the gunge clung to Mark's trainers. He bent down to wipe it off. It moved. It was a big fat worm.

"Hello, worm!" Mark muttered. "What's your name, eh? I'm Mark Spark. And you're . . . Wilfred."

"Have you gone completely crackers, Mark?" said Jason. "Why are you talking to your trainers?"

"And for my best birthday present

I'm getting a tent. I want a pink one,
because it's my favourite colour,"
said Louise. "And my mum says for
my birthday treat I can have some
friends to stay over night and we can
all sleep in my tent out in the garden.
Won't that be great?"

"You bet!" said Jason. "We can
come, can't we, Mark and me? We're
your friends, aren't we, Mark?"
Suddenly he noticed that Mark was
holding something. "What's that
you've got in your hand?" he asked.

"It's my new pet. Say how do you do to Wilfred." Mark held Wilfred up so he could maybe waggle his tail.

"YUCK!" Louise squealed, and she went flying down the road in her frog wellies.

She screamed so loudly that Mark jumped and dropped Wilfred back in the puddle.

"Oh Wilfred, come back!" said Mark. "Louise, you are a bore. You've made Wilfred run away."

Louise was still running away herself. "You keep that horrid worm away from me," she shrieked. "If you bring it anywhere near me again I won't let you stay overnight in my tent."

"It's okay, Louise," said Jason,

dashing backwards and forwards between them. "He's dropped his worm. So we can still sleep in your tent, eh?"

"Bye bye, Wilfred," said Mark sadly, stirring the muddy puddle in vain.

"Don't you dare fetch it out again!" Louise shouted.

"I can't. You've frightened him away," said Mark, sighing. He squelched along the road. "I don't know why you don't like worms, Louise. They're your favourite colour. Pink."

"Is your birthday tent really going to be pink, Louise?" asked Jason.

"Yep, with a pink sleeping bag to match. You and Mark will have to bring your own sleeping bags for my birthday treat," said Louise.

"No problem," said Jason.

Mark Spark didn't say anything. He did have a little problem. No, not a little problem. A Great Big Problem.

Chapter Two

Mark Spark didn't know what he was going to do. He didn't say anything to Jason. He didn't say anything to Louise. He couldn't tell them about his Great Big Problem. They might laugh at him. They would think he was a silly baby. Just thinking about it made Mark blush Louise's favourite colour.

Mark Spark had always had this Great Big Problem but he had kept it a deadly secret so far. Mark Spark was afraid of the dark.

He wasn't frightened of anything else. He'd dare anything. He didn't care about getting into trouble. He didn't cry when he fell and gashed his head and had to have ten stitches at the hospital. He didn't flinch when a pit bull terrier barked and tried to bite him. Everyone thought Mark Spark was the bravest boy in the whole school.

But he was still scared of the dark. He had a little lamp at home. Mum always left the hall light on too, in case he had to nip to the bathroom in the night. But even in the light he knew the dark was there, in all the other rooms. It was outside the windows, this huge terrifying darkness.

He knew he'd never be able to sleep outside in a tent with Jason and Louise. He could have a torch but that would be just a very little light in the very big darkness outdoors. It would be much much much too scary. Mark Spark might end up blubbing like a baby.

Great Gran guessed something was wrong when Mark went to her house for his tea.

"I've mucked up my new trainers, Great Gran," said Mark.

Great Gran was blind so she couldn't see them. But she could feel them.

"You mucky pup," she said. "We'd better give them a good wash, eh?"

Great Gran sorted out Mark's trainers as best she could.

"But there's still something wrong, duck," she said. "Can't you tell your Great Gran?"

"Well, I lost my pet worm Wilfred coming home from school," said Mark.

"Did you, dearie? How tragic," said Great Gran. "Still, I dare say you'll find yourself another worm. You could go out in my back garden and get one right away. How about a lady worm this time? Wilma Worm?"

"Yes, good idea, Great Gran," said Mark, but he didn't sound enthusiastic.

"There's still something bothering

my little lad," said Great Gran, and
she reached out for Mark and pulled
him onto her lap. "What is it,
chum?"

"Oh Great Gran!" Mark wailed.
"I don't know what to do. Louise is
getting a tent for her birthday and
she's asked me and Jason to stay
overnight to camp in her garden and

I can't because . . . because . . .
because I'm scared of the dark."
Mark said it in a very little voice.
Great Gran was rather deaf as well
as blind but she heard him and she
hugged him tight.

"Don't you fret yourself, my pet.
We'll sort something out, just you
wait and see."

Chapter Three

"I'm ever so sorry, Louise," said Mark. "I really wish I could stay overnight for your birthday treat. But I can't. I've got to go and stay with my Great Gran that weekend."

"Oh Mark!" said Louise, frowning. "Don't muck up my birthday treat."

"Can't you go and stay with your Great Gran some other weekend?" said Jason. "You've *got* to come too, Mark."

"I'm sorry. But I've got to be with Great Gran. She's – she's scared of the dark, you see. She needs me there," said Mark.

"Hang on," said Jason. "Your Great Gran's blind, so she's always in the dark. Why should she be scared?"

Mark Spark scratched his head. "Burglars," he said. "There've been several break-ins down near my Great Gran's. She's getting nervous."

It was true enough. There had been several burglaries. And Great Gran *was* worried about it. And Mark Spark certainly wanted to look after her. Great Gran always looked after him. It was her idea that he should stay with her, so he needn't go to stay with Louise.

"It won't be any fun without you, Mark," said Jason.

"Yes it will," said Louise crossly. "Okay then, Mark. If you can't come I'll invite my friend Lily instead."

"Yuck! Not *Lily*," said Jason,

looking horrified. "I can't stick Silly Lily."

Jason didn't ever dare call Lily Silly to her face. She might have a small soft name but she was a big tough girl and she never let any of the boys boss her about. But she could be good fun too. She often had good ideas. Almost as good ideas as Mark Spark.

It was very hard for Mark
listening to Louise and Jason and
Lily planning the birthday treat.

"Mum says we can cook food on
her little camping stove," said
Louise.

"Sausages! Wow, can we have
sausages?" said Jason.

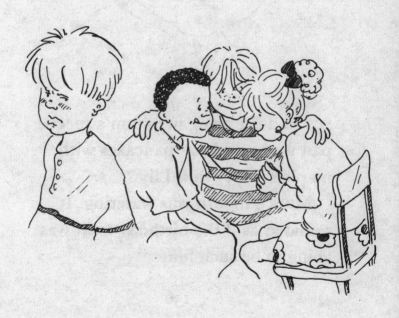

"And if I bring my mum's special pan we could have pancakes with maple syrup," said Lily.

Mark's mouth was watering. It sounded as if the birthday treat was going to be such fun.

"Look, Louise, maybe I could come for the camp stove feast?" he said hopefully. "Then I could go along to my Great Gran's after, when it gets dark and you lot go to bed in the tent."

"No, Mum says I can only have two friends. She says more will just get silly. And now I've asked Jason and Lily," said Louise.

"Lily *is* silly," Jason muttered to Mark. "Hey, I do wish you were coming instead of her, Mark."

"So do I," said Mark miserably.

It was hard when he knew he wasn't going because *he* was the silly one.

Chapter Four

"We'll have our own camp fire feast, little pal," said Great Gran on Saturday night.

Mark helped her cook it in the kitchen. They had sausages. They had bacon too. And baked beans. And chips. They didn't eat it at the kitchen table as usual. They went into Great Gran's lounge and she switched her electric fire on, even though it was a hot evening.

"It's our camp fire, right?"

159

said Great Gran.

"You bet," said Mark, sitting down cross-legged in front of the fire.

Great Gran couldn't quite manage to sit cross-legged, but she drew her armchair up near the fire and they had their feast. Then they had their pudding.

"Oh Great Gran!" said Mark, seeing the bowl of batter. "Are we having pancakes too?"

"You bet," said Great Gran.

She cooked the pancakes in very hot fat. They made a lot of smoke. It was very like a camp fire. Great Gran couldn't see but somehow she knew exactly when to toss each pancake. She made six. She ate two. Guess who ate four. One with lemon and sugar. One with jam. One with chocolate spread. And one with condensed milk.

Mark Spark felt very full indeed afterwards. He watched television with Great Gran but the heat from the fire and the food in his tummy made him feel very very sleepy.

"Come on, we're both nodding off," said Great Gran. "Let's go to bed, eh?"

They got undressed and Mark
cleaned his teeth and Great Gran
popped hers in an old cup in the
bathroom. Then they both climbed
into Great Gran's bed.

"We can play tents in here," said
Great Gran, pulling the bedclothes

over their heads.

"No, it's a bit too dark, Great Gran," said Mark.

"Okay pet," said Great Gran, tucking the sheets back under Mark's chin.

She said Mark could keep the light
on all night long. Mark snuggled up
happily, feeling safe. Great Gran was
especially cuddly without her corsets.
Mark fell asleep straight away.

He had a funny dream about
Louise and Jason and Lily. They
were all safe in their tent with
torches but they'd pushed him out in
the dark and he didn't know what to
do. He stumbled around in his
dream, bumping into things and

crying. He heard himself wailing and then he heard Great Gran's voice.

He woke up. He felt for Great Gran. He sat straight up in bed. Great Gran wasn't there! He heard the weird wailing again. And then he heard Great Gran's voice outside, down in the garden.

What was she doing out there in the dark by herself?

Mark started shivering, wishing Great Gran would come back. Then he heard a thump and a bang and a fumble and a groan. Great Gran!

Was it a burglar? Had he hurt Great Gran?

"You leave my Great Gran alone!" Mark Spark shouted, and he hurtled out of bed, out of the bedroom, down the stairs three at a time, down the passage and out the back door. Into the dark. The great black terrifying outdoor dark.

"Great Gran!" Mark shouted, scarcely able to see a thing. And then he bumped right into someone and shrieked.

"Hey, little darling, it's only me," said Great Gran, holding him tight. "What are you doing out in the garden, eh?"

"What are *you* doing out in the garden?" Mark gasped. "Where's the burglar?"

"There's no burglar, sweetheart. Just a silly cat who's been rooting around in my dustbin. I just tripped right over it. But I think we've frightened him off now."

"Good."

"So you thought there was a burglar? And yet you came out here in the dark to protect your old Great Gran, eh? That was very very brave of you."

Mark thought about it. "Mmm. Yes. I suppose it was," he said, pleased.

"The dark isn't so very terrible, is it?" said Great Gran.

Mark looked all around him. It wasn't so bad now he was holding Great Gran's hand. It wasn't really so frightening at all. It wasn't even as black as he'd expected. Maybe he'd be able to stay over at Louise's house next time.

He looked up at the dark sky and smiled.

"I can see all the stars, Great Gran," he said. "They sparkle."

"Like you, pet. My Markle Sparkle," said Great Gran.

Where there's trouble, there's bound to be

Bad Becky

But you can't help loving her!

After all, wouldn't you prefer to hear a story about a princess-gobbling dragon than some soppy fairy tale?

Very good stories about a BAD little girl!

The furry bundle has arrived.

'Okay, okay. So hang me. I killed a bird. For pity's sake, I'm a cat.'

Get your claws out for the hilarious antics of Tuffy and his family as told by the killer cat himself. If you know cats, you'll understand.

'Infectiously funny and highly readable' – Independent

Cover illustrations © Steve Cox

'A brilliant tale of catastrophe and pussy pandemonium' – Daily Telegraph

Lily Quench

Thirsty for a magical adventure?

Let Lily Quench it!

She's a feisty young dragon slayer and she's ready for action. Get ready for some scorching adventures in this exciting series.

lilyquench.com

An ordinary girl with EXTRAORDINARY plans!

Recipe for Disaster

Take:
- One ten-year-old girl with big plans
- One opportunity to appear on TV

Leave to marinate

An ordinary girl with EXTRAORDINARY plans!

Alexandra the Great

What's Cooking, Alex?

YVONNE COPPARD

Stir in:
- One oversized dog
- One gorgeous celebrity chef
- One arch-enemy

Bake at a high temperature

Serve with a big smile and hope for success!